270

A Novella

IAN SCHRAUTH

Pocket Reads

HeartStone Virtual Solutions, LLC

To purchase in bulk at a discounted rate, please contact HeartStone Virtual
Solutions: heartstonevirtualsolutionsllc+bulkpurchasw@gmail.com

Paperback ISBN: 978-1-0881-8816-3
eBook ISBN: 978-1-0882-2802-9

Paperback edition printed and bounded by IngramSaprk
Kindle edition distributed by IngramSaprk

Pocket Reads is an imprint of HeartStone Virtual Solutions, LLC

PREFACE

CHAPTER 1

Great…

Where do I start THIS time?

I was doing drive through at Taco Bell on the last day of school. It was – of course – Tammy, Keith, and I.

And it was packed….

While I was taking someone's order, I heard someone yell at me.

Now, the *Franchise* made a rule just for me…if they call me gay, I have full permission to tell them off.

AFTER they made me a manager!

That's right bitches!

I'm a fucking manager!

And not just *any manager!*

An assistant!

Gotta love them!

"Hey! Can I have a waffle?" he asked.

I looked at him, and looked back.

"I'm, talking to you!"

"Three fifty please full forward." I said in the speaker and sent the order.

I walked over to the guy, and faced him. "If you want a waffle, you can go get one at the waffle house. We don't *serve* them *anymore.*"

He looked offended. He was only 15, so he was probably just joking.

"What's up with you? Uncut dick up your ass?"

Well, that's a new one!

He talked like a creep! Like he was trying to hit on me, but failing miserably.

"No?" I asked. "Aren't those for fuckboys?"

"No, they're for fags like you."

OK, now I know he's starting shit...

"Sir, you're speaking to a manager here." I said and showed him my name tag that said "Gary Heckerson, assistant manager"

"Wow! Can fagboy get me some free tacos?" he asked.

"No, but you can get me your receipt." He said.

Keith took the hint, so he took over drive through.

"No."

I fiddled around with the computer, and pulled up his order, and issued a refund. I handed him the money, and said, "Have a good day."

"Man, I want my food!" he companied.

"Well, you're not going to get your food with an attitude like that. Now will you?"

"You seem like the type that fucks men."

"If I *do*, at least I could consider myself sexually active. And no, your hand doesn't count. Now, get the fuck out of my restaurant."

The customer started to go behind the counter. This was a HUGE safety threat, because he had a pocket knife.

Keith saw this, and paused said to the next customer in his ear, "Please hold."

I heard the customer complain, but I didn't care.

I pressed a button under the register, and that instantly locked all the doors.

Not only does it lock doors...

It also notifies the police to get here ASAP.

"Fuck with me faggot and you die!" he said and started to walk towards me.

"GET AWAY FROM HIM YOU BASTARD!"

I thought that was a customer...

But no...

It was TAMMY! Walking up to him with a PICO KNIFE!

Damn...talk about releasing her inner serial killer!

Have you seen those things?

They're HUGE!

The boy started to walk towards her, with the knife facing outwards. Even though his knife was smaller, his was a LOT Sharper!

That thing looked like it could give the air more than just a slice!

Tammy backed off a little, but he kept going.

I started to go after him, but when he pointed her to a wall, I could feel myself be shoved out of the way, and I could hear bodies clomp to the floor...

Multiple...bodies...

CHAPTER 2

It made news.

"15 year old robs Taco Bell"

And yeah, he tried to ROB us! He confessed to it to authorities...

And he stated, "I offended him"

Bitch!

If you're offended, then leave! Don't go on a fucking killing spree for some free tacos!

I was watching the full media coverage on the news with my sister, and mom that same day, and they looked shocked. Not only that they interviewed me, but also that I almost got killed.

"As long as you're safe." Mom said and started to cry a little.

Before I could say anything, there was a news interruption...this was not any new interruption...

It was from the President.

Jarmen McMiller.

I do not like him at all...I mean, he's just a snotty republican disguised as a communist that wants to ban LGBT rights, raise taxes, and make us gay people's rights revoked.

I like what former Democratic President Sanya Comdisk did...

She made anything related with LGBT rights LEGAL in all 50 states!

I didn't want to even look at that man's face. He was a shame to the LGBT community...he vowed to protect us, and now he's destroying us.

I'm just glad of one thing...

The 2016 election is coming up soon.

"I think that this is just a sad situation. I mean, why you even rob a TACO BELL? Rob something good!" president Jarmen asked. "What a shame"

And before he could say anything, the TV shut off.

"I can't stand that fucker!" Mom complained and got up. "He's a disgrace to our party."

OUR party?

I'm an independent!

I want the government out of our lives, out of our taxes, and out of our bedrooms.

But then again, I don't care for politics, so I don't do my research...

Is what I believe an ACTUAL party?

Who knows...

Jenny and I both got up, and headed to our rooms.

"Hey, at least his term is almost up." Jenny said and sat down on her bed. "The RNC and DNC are coming up."

Yeah…

We'll probably have two shitty candidates…

PART ONE
ONE YEAR LATER

CHAPTER 3

It was the first day of our school newspaper meetings before school officially starts. I wanted to be here SO badly...

Even though it is four days until it starts...

I was getting bored with the life of "home".

I didn't have class until two, so I headed to the newsroom to relax.

Let me rephrase that....

Relax!

And not be worried about Connor coming in and making my heart race.

He moved to bigger and better things.

I forgot what university he went to – It was somewhere in New York – But knowing him...he probably enrolled in Bust-A-Nut university.

When I walked in, I sat my backpack in my seat, and sat down on the couch.

"Hey Gary," I heard a voice announce.

It was our new Editor-in-chief, Roman.

When I say Roman is probably going to be trouble, believe me.

Roman is Connor's twin brother.

He doesn't know about me.

And I hope he never gets the chance to know the truth...

"Hey Roman." I replied and walked up to me. Roman was hot...but I would never give into him.

He handed me a piece of paper, and said, "We need someone to report on this. It would be perfect for the first issue!"

I took a look at the piece of paper, and the title bored me.

** Libertarian National Convention held in the gym **

Eww...

Politics...

But I do have one question...

How is our leader chosen?

I could do this and find out...

"I'll do it!" I announced.

He looked at me and smiled.

That smile...

That damn smile...

Looks like the disgusting face of Connor's...

Yuck...

"Good! You do know it's four days long." He replied.

Jesus Christ!

"I know."

"Good! They start at twelve every day, and they will be nominating the president and vice president. As well as the chairman."

Well...

Let this political madness begin...

CHAPTER 4
DAY ONE

They let me in without an invitation because of my press pass, and *my god*. I know the gym is unusually large, but damn!

This place was fucking huge!

There were a fuckton of people EVERYWHERE!

A lot of tables with state names showing, and people sitting there.

They had a place for the press to sit, a group of chairs by the wall. It seemed uncomfortable, but we had a GREAT view!

I got some pictures of the crowd, and out of the blue, they all started to applause.

I looked up at the stage and I had to instantly get some pictures.

The current chairman of the Libertarian party just walked up!

He looked like a businessman. Not the fat ones though. He had jet black hair, and the face of a snob.

"Welcome to the 2016 Libertarian national convention!" he announced. "I am the chairman, Dr. Gonzala Black. I just have some stuff to say first."

He announced some stuff about the Libertarian party, and some goals, while I took some pictures. He looked very happy to be speaking.

After he was done, he thanked us, and as he was walking off, the room went into another round of applause.

Then a larger one…

The lady who walked out on stage even gave me chills.

That woman was the one and only Ava Frank.

Even though she was on her way to the grave, she was the first woman to receive an electoral college vote in history.

And also the first atheist.

And yes, she's a Libertarian.

I did my research.

She slowly made her way up to the podium, and I took as many good pictures as I could. I mean, who wouldn't want to miss this moment?

When she reached the podium, everyone continued to clap, and a lot of people stood up. She was like their hero.

Probably because she is a figurehead in the Libertarian party.

When they died down, she started to give a speech. She tanked us all for coming, said some stuff about herself, a then the magic stared…

Oh…

My…

God…

Her speech was really good! Not because of her grandmother-like voice, but word after word was carefully planned out, forming a very uprising speech.

It kind of got me thinking.

Maybe I should get involved with politics. Not a whole lot, but a little.

When I got done taking photos, Ava stopped speaking, tanked us, and walked off the stage. We were left with a blank stage, until Dr. Gonzala Black came back up, and started to introduce the candidates.

The presidential candidates.

The ones who will fight to be chosen to represent the Libertarian party.

One by one, they started to come up, and Dr. Gonzala Black explained their background. One of them was Judith Vargas, a former governor of Utah, another was Mary Stone, a Representative from Missouri, one was some unknown Libertarian activist, and one of them I knew VERY well.

Dillon Derid.

The owner of Derid software inc!

His company creates mock applications that are meant for Ubuntu.

His company is well known in the Linux community.

I have to interview him!

These were all of the candidates who made it passed all of the other debates. They have been debating for a long time, and many of them have dropped out.

Now it's time to show their true potential.

The questions were asked by the moderator, former Libertarian presidential candidate from 2008, Jack Justman.

But they had to ask one question before they were allowed to debate.

"What does it mean to be a Libertarian?"

All the candidates basically said the same answer, "Legalize a lot of things, and give us freedom." But Mary Stone gave one of the best answers.

"We believe in freedom. We believe in a government should stay out of our personal life's! They should let us marry who we want to marry! We should live how we want! If we want to get high, let us! If we want to give ourselves a piercing in places we want, let us! And most of all, if we want to identify as a different gender, we should do so!"

And that made everyone cheered!

From someone that isn't into politics, it got me so interested!

There were some more pre-debate questions, like taking away votes from the Republican Party and how they feel about it, about the presidential debates later on, and one thing that makes them different from the rest.

Mary rocked it...again.

She said that she would get our troops out of war, save money on military spending, and use that money to create jobs, give tax breaks, and make the economy green!

Oh wow...

When the pre-questions (and the many pictures I took) were done, the real debate started.

***

The debates were over. A lot of people were excited, and I was able to go backstage to interview some of the candidates.

But I kindly interviewed Dillon.

When I returned to the newsroom, Roman was gone, and a lot of editors were talking.

"We saw you on TV Gary." The new opinions editor, Chloe, said.

What?

"How?" I asked.

"You were taking a photo."

Oh...

"Speaking of that..." is and went to my computer. I plugged in my SD card, and pulled up the files. "I got a total of 783 pictures."

Yes...

I got THAT many.

The new News editor, Chad, walked over to my computer, and took a look with me.

"These are good! We could use these for the paper, and the online portfolio!" he said. "These stories your writing is going online only."

Oh...

He walked away, and I wrote my story.

CHAPTER 5

When I got home, the story was online. Mom was making a late diner, and it smells…DELECIOUS!

"HI mom." I said and sat my backpack on the couch.

"Hey Gary!" she yelled from the kitchen.

I walked in, and sat down with my laptop. I opened it up, and looked at my online story.

And just as I guessed, mom noticed.

"The Libertarian national convention at your school?" she asked, surprised. "Wow! It must have been a privilege being able to go there!

It was!

"They have the next debate tomorrow, and I'm expected to cover it." I announced. "Then after the convention, they take a break until the primaries."

"Oh yeah! Those are next week!" mom said. "Did you register to vote?"

Yes…

"Yes I did." I replied.

"Good! I hope you vote for who YOU like." Mom said and grabbed something out of the cupboard.

She went back to make her meatloaf, and I took a look on the Libertarian website to see what the higher-ups thought.

They were all predicting that Mary Stone would be the nominee.

I don't blame them!

I think she rocked the performance!

but the fact that surprised me is that there were current representatives trying to get the nominations. And I know that those were the ones who identified as a republican.

Secretly, they want to be with the Libertarian.

I looked back at the page, and I noticed that I got a comment.

** Better than the RNC candidates! **

Wait...

Who ARE the candidates?

I went to Google and searched for the candidates...and dear god did I regret it...

I found that not only there were 13 other people trying to run, but also one of them was president Jarmen.

And from a poll, he was the most popular one out of the bunch...

Great…

I look at mom, and said, "Hey, president Jarmen is leading in the republican polls."

She slowly turned around, anger staring at my face. I could tell she did NOT want him to win.

"I hate that man. He is a disgrace to our party. I hope he doesn't get re-nominated!" she said and turned back around.

Damn…

I knew she hates him, but not that much.

I know Americans are way to attached to their political parties, but I fell like this president is crossing into different territories.

I feel like he's crossing out of republican territory, and into the Constitution party.

You know, the party that makes republicans look left-wing?

Yeah…

I closed my laptop, and headed up to my room. my room was a complete fucking mess.

Clothes all over the floor, chords everywhere, and college papers all over.

Typical for a college student.

I sat my backpack on my desk, and as I was about to change into my PJs, I got a message.

From Jordan.

As you know from last year, we got back together. I told Connor to go fuck himself (he probably did) and told the advisor about what was going on.

Long story short, he got fired, and graduated early.

he was only staying that semester to be on The Gossip.

I picked up my phone, and texted him.

CHAPTER 6
DAY TWO

I woke up, and got on some new clothes. I had to go to the second day of the LNC, and I was ready.

I was thinking all night about who would win.

I think it will be Mary.

I checked my phone, and I saw a message from Jordan. He sent this about five minuets ago.

** Get up cumdumpster! I'm taking you to school! **

I have no fucking idea what got into him, but he's been calling me that for the past week.

Maybe he wants me to be his cumdumpster...

Eww...

Not after what happened with Connor.

Yuck...

I got my camera, press pass, and notebook, and headed outside. It was nice out.

I mean *NICE*! The weather was just down right perfect!

If only they could have the convention outside.

I saw Jordan pull up, and he honked a little. I was just staring off into space.

I got in his car, and put on my seatbelt. "What's up."

He smiled at me, and while pulling out, he said, "If I tell you, you'll have to sit on it."

"Not while driving I wont! you need to see what your doing on the road."

he smirked at me. "Doesn't mean I want a hand job."

Just...stop...

"No, I'm not reaching my hand in your pants while your driving. Knowing you, you'll get an orgasm and crash into some old lady."

"Yeah, yeah, yeah."

***

When we arrived at school, we parked in the student parking space, and got out.

"Well, I'll see you later." I said and gave him a kiss.

The peaceful, romantic kiss lasted a little longer than expected, because he pulled off, and said, "OK, we better get in now."

~24~

We went our separate ways, and all I could think about was who would Jordan would vote for.

he's strange with his voting patterns, according to him.

He votes not based on his party, but based on what HE believes they will do.

Jordan is a one of LGBTQ Republicans, and he one time voted for the Green party.

They're, like, WAY far to the left.

That's not right!

Yeah, pun intended...

When I walked in, I could see everyone talking. It looked like they were about to start soon.

I took some good photos, and when I was finished, the first speaker came out.

This time, it was Will Georgia.

I don't know much about him, but I do know that he was the nominee for president last election.

He got one electoral college vote...from someone who was pledged to vote republican, but wanted freedom.

He introduced himself as the crowds cheered by his responses, and when he was done, the moderator announced the vice presidential candidates.

There were five of them this time.

Some of them were former representatives, one was the former governor of Washington, there was an an activist, and one was an author.

One of them stood out to me…

When all of the candidates were introduced, they stared with the same format as last time. Ask question go back with my press pass, answer, and then some type of argument on issues. There was some insulting going on, but nothing too bad.

All I can say was that I got a lot of pictures…but not much data for a story.

So, I decided to interview some of the candidates.

When the debates for the VP were over, there was a break time, and I decided to go back stage with my press pass, and interview just one of the candidates.

I decided to interview the former governor.

I walked up to him, and said, "Excuse me Governor Henrick?"

He turned around, and smiled at me. "Hi!"

"I'm with the school newspaper, called The Gossip, and I would like to interview you for a story. May I?" I asked.

"Sure. I used to work in Journalism, so you can record my answers."

Wow…

There's a question I could ask about!

We sat down in some chairs, and I got out my recorder.

***

Well, that went well.

We got into some REALLY good questions, and I got some REALLY good content for a story!

But I think I'll change it into a Q&A.

I went ahead and left the gym because they were just casting their votes, and I headed back up to the newsroom.

When I walked in, I saw Roman on his computer.

"Hey, how was the second day?" he asked.

"Good, I got an interview with one of the candidates, and I think I'll do a Q&A for this post."

He looked at me. "That would be perfect for a new online segment we're doing! It's a section on the website where we'll do Q&As with famous people every one in a while. Can you translate them for me?"

Translating…

The worst thing a journalist has to do…

"Sure," I replied and want to my computer.

While I was starting to set up my area, Roman got a call.

"Hey Connor, what's up?" he asked.

Let me go and kill myself now…

As I started to walk out of the room, Roman called me.

"Hey, my brother wants to speak to you. Do you know him?"

Uh…*yes* I know him…

"I do." I replied and walked up to him. I grabbed his phone, and as a placed the phone by my ear, I wanted to just die inside.

"Hello?" I asked.

"Hey Gary. How are you?"

Lord, please help me now…

"I'm good. How's New York?" I asked, trying to sound interested.

"Good. I just wanted to congratulate you for that piece on the LNC."

Why?

Why is he being nice to me now?

After he fucked me and dumped me…

"Thanks." I replied.

"So listen, I actually am coming back this weekend. Do you want to hang out?"

CODE RED!

HANG UP!

I hung up the phone, and handed it back to Roman.

"Everything OK?" I asked.

"He had to quickly leave." I replied and walked out.

God damn, I don't want to fall for that shit again...

CHAPTER 7

Right after I got done with the article, they called me in to work to help them close.

God damnit.

I hate that place.

I liked it before, but since I almost died, its gone down hill.

People are scared of coming in because they think there going to die.

They all come at night…

And I mean ALL of them.

And the franchise is cutting people. Even if the sore want it or not.

I almost got cut, but I'm the truck manager, and nobody else wants to do it.

Not even the General manager wants to do it.

It's why I still have that job there…

I arrived at the restaurant, and noticed that customers were wrapped around the building.

it was almost to the street!

I rushed in, and saw the lobby was packed. People looked angry as fuck.

I quickly clocked on, and rushed to the other side to make food.

"Thanks Gary!" Vince said.

"We've been this way for three hours." Tammy, who was the one who finished and wrapped the food, said.

Damn...

They probably had a bunch of panic attacks.

and probably have infections from holding their pee in.

I made a lot of the lobby's food. I went through it quickly. People seemed in a better mood when they got their food, and none of them were ass holes. I finished making their food before they got done in the drive through, and helped them.

***

The lobby was now locked.

We have three hours to do all of the dishes, and clean the line.

And that was exactly what I was doing.

When all the orders were done in the drive through, Vince decided to help me with the line, while Tammy did the dishes.

I was talking to Vince about the RNC candidates. We got into a little debate about our current president.

"No, I don't think he's racist at all. And I have proof!"

"Prove it."

"Well, first off, the media likes to say lies about him. For example, when he visited China, they said something rude about a Chinese tradition he did. And the fact that the butthurt liberals are still trying to get him impeached for lies that the media has said about him is sad. He had created more jobs, and cut programs that are just wasting money and are no longer needed for society. And surprisingly, studies show that there are a lot of immigrants with drugs. He only wants to stop THEM. He loves the diversity in our country. This country is nicknamed the melting pot, and he respects that. If you don't believe me, do the research."

Wow...

I didn't realize that.

If this were true, it would change my views about that guy.

But then again, he says stuff that makes me mad.

Like the shooting incident.

"Did you hear what he said about the shooting incident though?" I asked.

"Yes, and he was being funny. He tries to be, but fails a lot. He has a history of writing for comedians."

Wow...

Those comedians must have been horrible...

"Well, I'm not voting for him anyway. In fact, I'm not voting democrat either." I replied.

He just opened at me. "Who are you voting then?"

"Libertarian."

He just chucked a little while collecting some pans. "You're wasting your vote. Third parties never win."

Oh Vince, I have a feeling you're going to eat those words.

CHAPTER 8
DAY THREE

I woke up the next morning, ready for the next day. I REALLY wanted Mary to get the nomination.

But then again, I was thinking about what Vince had said last night.

No, I don't think he's racist at all. And I have proof!

I got up early enough, so I decided to the research.

I looked up many things on Google, but about thirty minuets later, I found something.

The website was from Fox news, and it was titled *Jarmen: the monster or not?*

after reading through it, I concluded that Vince was wrong.

But you can't trust the media these days...

***

When I reached the campus, I put on my press pass, and headed down to the gym. it was empty, except for Mary, and a vice presidential candidate.

They were talking.

I decided to just sit down in the journalism area, and wait. I didn't think they would notice me, because I was on my phone.

But I was listening...a little.

"If I pick you as my VP, you need to help me campaign. I would take the states that want Marijuana legalized and then some, and you'll take the rest. Ok?"

"Deal." he replied.

Crap.

What was his name again?!

I wrote down what he looked like, and soon, people were quietly piling in.

***

When everyone was in the gym, it was very talkative. I had to put on some headphones in order to concentrate on the book I was reading.

Someone was going around, collecting people's papers, and then went to the back.

there was an announcement from the chairman.

"Thanks for voting. We will count the ballots now, and the winner will speak!"

Shit!

they voted?!

I showed them my pass, and headed backstage to interview the chairman.

How did they count the ballots?

Did they print out the ballots at home?

Who does he think the winner is?

I need to find out!

I walked up to him, and explained I was on the school newspaper. "May I record your answers?" I asked.

"Yes!"

I set up my recorder, and began.

"Why did people have to hand in those papers?" I asked.

"Well, they did their votes electronically, but they had to print out a conformation piece to have their vote count. They put in the ID number on the op, and it'll say if the vote is legit or not."

Interesting...

"Do you think that you'll continue this system?"

"Yes, this is a new system, and we might upgrade it to take faster -- like with barcodes and a computer -- but we're most likely keeping it."

"Who do you think will be the winner?"

"Only time will tell."

Crap...

"If you were to give Libertarian 101 to someone, how would you start the lesson?"

"We want freedom everywhere, from your bedroom, to your body, to your lives. we don't want the government to mess and tease us, at all."

Wow…

That was good!

"Last question. Is there such thing as left-wing libertarianism?"

"Sort of. There's what we believe -- right wing -- and then there's the made up version that is not official -- left wing. They want more government, and to do a lot more in our lives. Some people follow what they call 'Libertarian green' and that's a combination of the green party, and the unofficial left-wing Libertarianism. I know, it doesn't make sense."

Well, that was good!

"OK, thank you." I replied and smiled.

I packed everything up, shook his hand, and walked out.

***

I was sitting where everyone else was, when the chairman came out.

"The votes have been counted. The winner is…" he stared as he pulled out a piece of paper.

Here we go!

"Mary stone!"

YES!

I feel like she strongly represents the Libertarian party!

Everyone broke out into a loud applause, with whistling and everything, as Mary came out to the stage.

I got some amazing photos, and she started with her acceptance speech as I pressed the RECORD button on the camera.

And I recorded the entire speech.

CHAPTER 9

The speech wasn't that long.

I mean, it was only for like, ten minutes, but still.

She got the fucking nomination!

And Fox even interviewed me!

I'll be on TV!

I was featured on the front page of the newspaper, but this is even better!

Ok, I'm getting off track…

When I typed up the document and posted the video to YouTube, I headed home, and went to my room.

I was tired and cranky.

I didn't want to deal with anybody for the rest of the night.

I have class tomorrow, and I have to get up early.

Shit…

I got on my PJs, and went to bed.

*****

When I arrived at school, I walked into my class, looking like I just got done having bomb-ass sex. My hair was not done, my clothes were sloped on, and I was overall horrible.

I hate getting up early...

I sat down in my American politics class.

I wanted to take this class to learn a little bit about politics, but not a lot.

But since that convention, I really want to learn more!

I sat my head down on the desk, and decided to take a quick nap.

But before I could close my eyes, the teacher, Professor Shela, walked in.

There goes that...

"Good morning class. Did you hear that The Gossip covered the Libertarian national convention that happened this week?" he asked.

That woke me up.

"I did sir." I replied.

"Gary? You did?" he asked.

Yeah?

"Yes. My name is on the articles." I replied.

He pulled up the articles to show us, and read them out loud to the class.

Why?

Why would you do that?

When he was done sucking my soul out, he stared to pass out papers.

When I looked at mine, I looked at the title.

<u>The start of the Democratic Party</u>

Great...

That's all I need to learn about...

I want to learn about something conservative! Like the formation of the Republican Party!

Or even better! The Libertarian party!

But we probably wont cover that.

It's a *third party*...

And he's against them...

But when they're on campus, he loves them...

Hypocrite!

He started to tell us about Andrew Jackson, and how they called him a donkey. And taxes this. And slavery that.

I hate the Democratic Party!

They want taxes!

And that's bad!

AND THEN THERE'S BUTTHURT LIBERALS!

They wouldn't stop rioting because President Jarmen got elected.

FOR THREE DAMN YEARS!

JESUS CHRIST!

CALM THE FUCK DOWN!!

But wait a minute…

We're still talking about the Federalist Party and the Democratic-Republican Party!

Why is he skipping!

When he got done talking, I confronted him.

"Why are we skipping?" he asked.

"Good question! It's because Phill Pozman is going to accept his nomination for the Democratic Party ticket! Aren't you guys excited?"

NO!

I'm NOT!

That guy is a pornstar, turned social media star, turned senator, turned presidential candidate!

This is no joke; he is very close to a communist.

He has similar views to one.

I would prefer the other guy better. The Socialist democrat.

But noooooooo!

They had to go with the one who more than held the country has seen his dick!

Eww!

"No, I don't want to vote for a porn star." I replied.

He just glared at me. "It doesn't matter what has happened in his past! All that matters is his political past!

"That makes no sense! If things don't matter in his past, that INCLUDES the political side!" Roman, who was in my class, explained.

"Exactly. So basically, he's a nobody." I replied.

"He's done more good than bad!"

Oh god...

He's a liberal...

"It's actually the opposite." I replied. "He's done porn, pranked people on YouTube, put communist views in our congress, and tried to pass COMMUNIST laws!" I explained.

"He's NOT a good person!" Roman said.

"You know what? Get your Nazi views out of my class. You can drop out while you're at it!" he demanded.

We both got our things, and walked out.

"Now what?" I asked Roman.

He pulled out his phone, and pressed on the screen. "I'm showing this recording to president Jordan and Chancellor Farnem."

Damn!

He recorded it!

"We can also do a news piece once it goes viral!" I replied.

"It's probably won't go viral, but we can do an opinion piece."

YES!
Time to kick some liberal ass!

CHAPTER 10

"So, let me get this straight! He kicked you out because of your political beliefs?" president of the campus, Dr. Lisa Stein, asked.

"Yup." I replied.

"He had very liberal point of views, and we have conservative."

She rubbed her hands over her eyes, and said, "We've had problems with him before doing this. This must stop now."

Roman and I looked at each other, and it looked like we had the same idea.

Interview time!

I pulled out my notebook, and asked, "may I interview you about that?"

"Sure. That *would* be a good story!"

We bother pulled out our equipment, and before we could start, we heard a knock.

"Madam, we have another guest who got kicked out."

Her eyes opened wide.

"Well, have them come in!"

She came in, and we asked her if she wanted to be interview.

She agreed, and it started.

***

Politics professor faces impeachment.

That was the title of the cover story of the next issue.

Coming out next week.

Roman and I were able to write two different pieces -- one about the students getting kicked out and the other about him...and how me night be fired.

She had a talk with him.

She's thinking about firing him!

When I arrived home, I went straight to my room, and laid on my bed.

All I wanted to do was be lazy!

I unlocked my phone, and looked at my emails.

One from the school

"Dropped class notice"

Shit...

THIS isn't good!

Dear student:

The following class (es) have been dropped from your schedule.

Intro to American politics: Pr. Kevin Shela

You now have the following classes on your schedule.

None

The reason for the drop:

Disrupting the class with nonsense and not listening to directions.

WHAT?!

He *DROPPED* me?!

how could he?!

I can't be on the school newspaper if I'm dropped!

I need to contact Dr. Lisa Stein!

I went to my computer, and wrote up a quick email.

Dr. Stein,

I have forwarded you an email that contains proof that I have been dropped from my class. I don't know if roman has or not, but this needs to be fixed.

Thanks,

Gary Heckerson.

Now, time for bed!
But not before a notification on Facebook from Roman.

Were u dropped from the class? I was...

Shit!
He was too!

Yes.

We need to email Dr. Stein.

Already did.

Good. I'll talk to her tomorrow.

CHAPTER 11

I had to *work* today.

Ugh!

I hate that place!

But anywhere else ain't any better!

I arrived at work, and went to the break room

"Hi Gary!" Vince said as I walked passed the line.

"Hey Vince."

"Hey, I want to congratulate you."

Huh?

"Why?" I asked.

"Your success on the school newspaper. I saw the posts!"

Wow!

He *reads* them?

Well shit!

"Thanks!" I thanked.

"You should endorse Mary, because I think you agree with her."

I never thought about that!

"I think I will!" I said.

"She now has a website, and I saw if you buy some of her merchandise, you automatically endorse her."

Well, I could use a "Mary for president" shirt!

But wait...

She hasn't even chosen a running mate!

"Do you know anyone who would be her running mate?" I asked.

"I don't know. if you need to reach out to her to find out, you can ask her. she loves it when student journalists reach out to her. I know that because she was the first libertarian to be in the US senate."

Wow...

the first...

I had some time before I clocked on...

why don't I post on her Facebook fan page my thoughts?

I walked to the break room, and typed up a message for her.

** Hey Mary, I interviewed you for the school newspaper during the convention. I have a recommendation for a vice presidential candidate if you want to hear it. **

I sent the message, and before I left he break room, I got a response.

** Great! That could be a great opinion piece! if you want to, we can talk about it. email my campaign manager at Promotion@maryStone2016.com! **

After I clocked on, I headed to the line, and helped them.

***

Holy shit.

It was crowded today.

Tammy had a panic attack it was so bad!

We ha d a fucking thousand dollar hour!

Like, HOW?!

I clocked off, and headed dot my car. Tammy's car had broken down, and I had to take her home.

When we got in the car, I started it up, and asked, "So, about Justin."

"Yes, he is the campaign manager for Mary Stone." she instantly said.

SHIT!

It's true!

"How did he get convinced and chosen?" I asked as I drove out of the parking lot.

"He's going for marketing in college, and he is related to Mary. She's his aunt. He's an I intern for her."

Wow!

"Well, I plan on voting for her." I replied.

"If you want, I can tell her about you and maybe make you her publicist."

"I have to interview her later."

"I can help. I mean, you are my BFF."

"Thanks!" I thanked.

Maybe I could do this for a living.

CHAPTER 12

the next day I headed to the newsroom, and sat down at my computer. I pulled up my email, and stared an email to Justin.

Dear Justin,

This is Gary, I am a friend with tammy. Mary told me to contact you for her email address and an interview. I am on the Gossip, the school newspaper.

Thanks,

Gary Heckerson.

I sent the email, and pulled up the dashboard to the website.
One new message!
From Mary!
I pulled up the message, and read it.

Dear Gossip staff,

My name is Mary Stone, Libertarian presidential candidate and US representative. I would like to be a guest writer for your paper. I had talked to Gary about some stuff, and he is going to write something else about me. If you could remind Gary, and have the Editor in chief contact my publicist   for   more   info   at JustinBrownPromotion@maryStone2016.com, we can talk.

Thanks,

Mary Stone.

Wow!

She wants to be a guest writer for OUR newspaper?!

Why ours though?!

That's strange…

I copied the message and screenshot it, and sent it to the advisor, editor in chief, and production manager.

They were pleased to hear!

Roman: Yes! we can have her as a gust writer!
Paul: What's this about Gary interviewing her?

Gary: she wants me to do an opinion piece on which I think would be a good vice presidential candidate. If it's not published here, I would publish it on my website.

Paul: We can do it online-only.

Gary: :-)

When I looked back at my email, I noticed a email back from Justin...

Hey!

Thanks for contacting me Gary. Don't worry, I know who you are, (Your Tammy's BFF). Mary is good for an interview today if you wish. at two o'clock. I can schedule you for then if you wish.

And by the way, Mary has something else she wants to talk to you about. I don't know what it is, but she just said that.

Her email is AdminMaryStone@marystone2016.com

Thanks,

Justin brown.

Did Tammy already tell her?

Wow...

That was quick.

I typed up the email to Mary, and decided tot take a nap.

Damn, I was tired...

CHAPTER 13

DING!

Shit…

A notification…

I was just about to go to sleep, when my phone rang.

I got up from the couch, and rubbed my eyes. I was tired as fuck…

I looked at my phone, and I noticed an email from Mary.

Hi Gary,

Thanks for contacting me! Go ahead and call me at two so we can do the interview.

She then listed her number, and I gave it a dial.

"This is Mary." she said as she picked up.

"Hi Mary, this is Gary. How are you?"

"I'm good! And you?"

"Good!" I replied and pulled out my questions. "Can I record your answers, just so I can get an accurate reading?"

"Sure!"

I pressed the record button, and started the interview.

"So, do you have a vice presidential candidate in mind?

"Sort of. I actually want to do a candidate that battled me at the debates my last election, but I don't know if he would say yes."

"Why don't you think so?"

"Well, we had some arguments going on, and long story short, he is now an independent."

"Did he get kicked out of the party?"

"Yes."

Wow…

"Who was this guy?"

"Just for privacy reason, I won't say."

"That's fine. Have you considered having Patience Ashmad as your vice presidential running mate?"

She was silent. "You mean the famous Libertarian activist?"

"Yup." I replied.

"No, I haven't. I'll look more into her." she replied. "It would take a two thirds vote from the Libertarian board to approve of her. And if they don't vote with me, it can be overturned by the PACs."

"I would recommend going with her," I replied. "She wants to have a government that is out of our lives, both economically, and socially. She has a strong belief in that, but has never run because of her past experience with politics."

"Gotcha."

"Another thing I want to ask is, what is your platform your running on?"

"Well, I'm mainly running on legalizing pot, and a plan I call "The tax reformation" That consist of revamping the tax system, making a unique tax based on each person's income, making social security privatized but mandatory.

I believe that people should give taxes to the government, but they have a choice on how much they give. I would make the minimum three dollars per paycheck to each department, that being the state, the protection force, and the government. If they want to do social security, they can opt out of it, but they will be known that they will be denied, as well as their kids. I would also make a new tax called "the green tax" where we would have people be taxed at their will to make our country convert to green energy."

Wow…

That's a weird, but interesting plan…

"Wow, that seems very interesting. Now, if you had a magic wand and could immediately change five things, what would they be, including legalizing pot, the green tax, and the tax reformation."

"Like you said, the green tax, pot, and taxes, but also cutting useless agencies, and achieving personal liberties, including ending the war on drugs, switching to a ranked voting system, and defending the second amendment, and keep in mind, BOTH leading candidates in the democratic and republican parities want to get rid of it! Jarmen and Jackson want to!"

Well shit!

I'm not a fan of the second amendment. I like it, but I think that they should monitor it more. But damn...

We shouldn't get rid of it all together...

"Do you think you have a shot at the white house this year? There has been no president who has been either a democrat or a republican since the Whig party."

"Yes, if I could be elected to the Missouri house twice, and the US house THREE times, then I can be elected president. I think I have a great marketing team to help me win. AND if we can maker it into the debates, that would increase our chances MAJORLY!"

True...

The debates almost decide who will win. It shows their beliefs.

It shows if they're qualified or not.

"True, if you can get over the 15%, you are qualified."

And if I am elected, I will require them to lower the percentage to under 10%."

Wow.

That will give more options!

We didn't have that since 1992 with Ross Perot, the independent running.

He didn't win....

"What do you think of the two leading candidates."

"Well, the DNC is about to choose Phill Pozman as their candidate, and it seems like Jarmen will be re-nominated. So, this is going to be a boxing match where one has leaked information and the other is racist against the other."

Wow...

Very descriptive...

"Well, those are all the question I have. What did you need to talk to me about?" I asked and stopped the recording.

"Well, Tammy had told me about you and how you were interested in being my publicist. Would you like to volunteer for a while, and then maybe become an intern?"

I KNEW IT!

YES!

"Sure!" I said.

"OK, I will email you some information you need to fill out, and some sites you need to join. Also, I will email you your new email to use with our website. You will need that email to register for the website. It has the info to use for the payments. OK?" Sure!

"OK!" I said excitedly.

"OK, I look forward to reading the opinion piece!" she said. "Have a good day."

"You too."

We hung up, and I just stared off into space.

Wow...

The chance to work with a presidential candidate to be her publicist!

I was excited!

When I went back to my computer, I wrote a post on the wall.

** Interview with Mary is complete! And she actually wants me to be her publicist for her campaign! I'm NOT joking around! **

I closed out of the web browser, and transcribed the interview.

CHAPTER 14
THREE DAYS LATER

I was sitting in the news room filling out some paperwork. I had to do this because Mary required me to.

Since I might be moving to an intern, I'll be getting paid for it.

And I would have to put it on my taxes.

Great...

It was giving me a headache. So...much...paperwork!

Dear god!

I decided to take a break and clear my head. I got up from my chair, and walked around the room.

God damn...

As I was about to lie down on the couch, I head Roman burst in.

Oww...

"Hey roman." I greeted and lay down.

"Hey, did you hear?" he asked.

Hear what?

"No?"

"Mary announced Patience Ashmad as her running mate! and she got the nomination!"

Well shit!

She took my advice!

I had looked up Patience yesterday, and she is, like, a god at marketing.

She knows how to get into people's emotions.

"I think I did something!" I said. My headache was fading now.

Probably from being excited.

"Why say that?" Roman asked.

"I recommended her to choose Patience Ashmad in the interview. Oh, and by the way. The article is up on the website."

"Wow!" Roman said and sat down at his computer. "They also announced that Jarmen and Phill Pozman has enough delegates to claim their ticket."

SHIT!

NOT HIM!

"Fuuuuuuuuuuuck." I replied and rubbed my face.

"Why the long fuck?"

Eww...

"First off...eww? And second off, I hate him."

"People don't give him enough credit for what he does. people lie about him, and poke fun at him. he's actually a REALKLY smart man, and I hate that people do that."

"I know that. I just don't like him because of the Taco Bell incident."

He looked confused. "What?"

"I was the manager in that store when that 15 year old tried to rob us. he said things that made me mad."

He looked angry. "Well shit! That's a good way to loose followers."

Well, I never liked him in the firs place, but I wont say that...

PART TWO
THE DEBATES

CHAPTER 15

Now, this election is a tough one. It's not like the last election, where Current president Jarmen McMiller of the Republican Party won. This election is different.

Nobody likes either the Democrat or the Republican candidates. If you forgot, the Democrats choose Regan Martin.

I like that name!

But he leaked secret information to Iraq when he was Secretary of State under Sanya Comdisk, and people can't trust him.

They want another option.

And that's where Mary Stone and Patience Ashmad of the Libertarian party come in!

There's a chance a she could win.

yeah, I was wrong.

In many states, including Kansas, Iowa, Colorado, the Dakotas, and her home state of Missouri, she is beating the two main candidates in the polls!

And another thing.

Many polls, including the Washington tomes and New York Times, state that Mary is Beating Jarmen!

She's in second!

And close to beating Regan!

Shit, at one time, she WAS beating them, but that was for about a couple weeks!

but still!

Because of our political past, the country is predicting that it's going to be a Republican victory.

I don't think so.

I'm hoping Mary deadlocks the Electoral College by winning enough states, and send it to the House.

The Republican congress will most likely pick Mary.

But maybe not Patience.

That's for the Senate to decide.

Why am I saying all this?

Well, because of her poling, Mary was invited to participate in the debates with Jarmen and Regan!

YES!

I was writing up a press release in my room when I heard a knock on my door.

"Come in."

Jenny came in.

"Hey, you got a letter from the school. I opened it for you, ad it says something about you being suspended.

WHAT?!

I grabbed the paper from her, and read it.

Gary Heckerson.

There has been a complaint made under your name regarding your behavior in one of your classes. According to the professor, you were: Disrupting the peace, hurting others, and saying lies to distract people.

According to Section 5[3], it states that any sort of action will be met with punishment, leading up to suspension, and termination of classes, credit hours, and jobs on campus.

Please meet with Regina Johnson on Thursday, September 7th at 2:45 at the main office to discuss this.

The following people will be there as well:

Professor Rod Shela
President Lisa Stein
Roman Kerth

Thank you,

Regina Johnson

WHAT?!

I was disrupting the peace in class?!

Bullshit!

"So, saying my opinion is disturbing the peace?" I asked Jenny.

"Apparently. Your piece on him kicking you out of class went viral. The *New York Times* even covered it!

Shit!

"That's probably why what they're going tot talk to you about." she said. "All I know is that this is America! the land of the free, including free speech!"

"I know!"

She walked out of my room, and I looked at the date.

September fifth...

The same day as the first debates.

I better find myself a lawyer so I can be prepared to sure this school!

They're NOT going to do this to me!

Mark my words!

CHAPTER 16
TWO DAY LATER

I was driving with Roman to the main office of the college. I was scared as hell.

I don't want to have any bullshit!

"Do you think the worst is going to happen?" Roman asked me.

"Hell yeah, knowing our luck."

We arrived at the campus, and we walked into the lobby.

"Can I help you?" the secretary asked.

I showed her the letter, and she directed us to Regena's office.

Before we could go in, we heard some screaming coming from the other side.

It was like an argument.

The voices sounded like President Stein, and someone else.

"Oh god." I said.

Roman nodded, knocked, and headed in.

There they were. Yelling at each other while Professor Shela was watching.

Regina, I think, looked at us, and said, "Ah, Roman and Gary! Come in!"

We walked in, and sat down into he chairs farthest from the professor.

"Now, we're here to talk about your actions in Professor Shela's class. We looked at the camera footage of the class, and talked to the witnesses, and I have conceded that you two will remain in your classes, but will be terminated from the Gossip.

OH HELL NO!

You son of a bitch!

"No, I do not apply with that. I have looked at the footage too, and concluded to terminate professor Shela." Lisa said.

"No, I am your boss, and I have the final say."

"I'm sorry, but the students have the right to appeal in cases like this, where the president agrees with the student's side. if I was agreeing with you, it would be different."

She just stared at her. "No, you do as I Say."

She pulled out her contract, and showed her to a specific page. "That section that we both agreed on when I was hired."

She snatched it from her hand, and read it. "No."

"No?" I asked. "That's all?"

"Yes, and that's the final answer."

Roman looked at me, held my arm, and got up.

I got a little bit of a boner. hey, I'm not goanna lie!

"Finem we will see you in court." he said as he dragged me out.

he dragged me to his car, and he stared to drive off.

"Seriously?" I asked. "Are we rally goanna sue?"

"Yup. Contact Paul and let him know."

***

"For Jarmen, and how we will continue to improve America...For Regan, and how we need to help America... And for Mary, and how we need to be the Change... From St. Louis, MO, this is the first presidential debates."

That was what the announcer had said.

We were watching the presidential debates at my house. My mother, X, jenny and I were very excited for this to start.

We were anxious...

"Good evening, and welcome to the first debates of three among the major candidates for President. The Commission on Presidential Debates sponsors the following three debates. This debate is different because we have three candidates with us instead of two. Representative from Missouri Mary Stone, the Libertarian nominee, Former Secretary of State Phill Pozman, the Democratic nominee, and President Jarmen McMiller, the Republican nominee. I am Lauren Buseremar of Fox News, and I will be the moderator for this 90-minute event, which is taking place before an audience in the athletic complex on the campus of Washington University in St. Louis, Missouri."

He went on and on about the rules, what they will be doing, blah, blah, blah...

Get to the good shit!

"The first question goes to Mrs. Stone. She will have 2 minutes to answer, to be followed by rebuttals of one minute each from Governor Jackson and then President McMiller. Ladies and Gentlemen, good evening."

YES!

"The first topic tonight is what separates each of you from the other. Mrs. Stone, what do you believe tonight is the single most important separating issue of this campaign?"

I could tell Mary was ready. She looked stunning, and proud. Ready to spread the Libertarian values, and have people on her side!

"First off, thank you for hosting the debates, and

thank you guys for coming to see us debate. I remember getting my degree in Political science here at this same school, and I am very proud of it. I think the main reason I am unique is that I am a candidate of Liberty. I represent a party that want to stay out of your lives. If you want to smoke what you want, do it! If you want to get married to your same-sex lover, I congratulate you on your wedding day. If you want us to stay out of your lives! We will do so! This is a party that came from people that wanted the government out of our lives, and the very first election, we made history, to have the first woman, and the first Jew, to receive an Electoral College vote.

This is the way the crafters of our great Constitution intended our government to be. That's why we all know the phrase "The land of the free." We have donkeys on the left that want to stay out of our lives socially, but not economically. Opposite for the elephants. Over the time, we have made a government who wants to be all up in our business. We need to back off, and let the people do as they wish, as long as it doesn't physically hurt anyone, or anything. Thank you."

Holy shit...

That was...like...REALLY good!

"Wow!" Jordan said. "That was great!"

"I know." I replied.

After Jackson and Jarmen gave their responses, but Jarmen said something that sparked interest.

"We have a candidate over there that wants to leak secrets to terrorist countries, and work behind our backs to kill us. We can't have a president who will do that! If I am in office, there will be a full search on Jackson, because he has risked many lives! Many hearts, and many souls! It's a disgrace, and you should be ashamed of yourself!"

Shit!

Shots fired!

"How do you respond to that, Senator Jackson?" Lauren asked.

"Well, I do have a good reputation. You are known for insulting people, and I'm glad that after this debate, because someone like you shouldn't be in charge of this country."

"Oh Madam secretary. If you were to be a better president, than Jarmen must be *better* than you. And I can tell you now. You both remind me a two pig race where one pig is a useless as it's shit and the other wants world domination." Mary added on.

SHIT!!!!

HOLY FUCK!

I had to laugh out lord at that one! Not only is Mary a freedom loving person, she's knows how to throw an insult! "Holy shit!" mom said and chuckled. "Shots fired!" I said.

After the crowd stopped applauding, Jarmen added on, "Look here, I'm not a candidate who wants to making everything from doing crack to raping kids legal here."

EWW!

WHY WOULD HE EVEN BRING THAT UP?!

GROSS!

"Eww." X said.

"Typical Jarmen." I replied.

Lauren interrupted, but Mary said before she could speak, "We have thousands of people in this world, and this is what the two main parties come up with? I'd expect more from a goldfish!" And the whole room went into cheering.

"Enough, we need to go on!" Lauren interrupted. "Starting with president Jarmen, the first question is as followed. Many people below in the middle class and below are being taxed twice as much as they were in Sonya's administration. The rich are getting richer by tax breaks, and the middle class is getting porrer. Do you have any tax cuts in mind to help the middle class?"

"Yes, I have thought through a new plan. We will make a plan that will have set tax for each level. The Middle class will be taxed less, and the higher classes will be taxed more. Some of the taxes will go to charities to help homeless people, and some will go to the government. It is a brilliant plan, and it think it would work very well in our society."

WHAT?!

"That's a horrible plan!" Jenny yelled.

"Jenny! Shush!" I replied.

"Mary, you have your two minuets."

"Well, unlike the other two, we have a better plan. I call it "the tax reformation." This consist of revamping the tax system, making a unique tax based on each person's income, making social security privatized but mandatory. I believe that people should give taxes to the government, but they have a choice   on   how   much   they   give.

I would make the minimum three dollars per paycheck to each department, that being the state, the protection force, and the government. if they want to do social security, they can opt out of it, but they will be known that they will be denied, as well as their kids. I would also make a new optional tax called "the green tax" where we would have people be taxed at their will to make our country convert to green energy. This is the true way to solve our tax problem, tax based on income, NOT social class!"

"I remember you saying that tax reformation plan to me, Gary ." X said. he started to inch his stand to my penis, but I slapped his hand.

"You're lucky mom went to the bathroom." Jenny said.

"I wanted to stroke that cock."

"Sorry, I'd rather not stroke a grain of rice."

JENNY!

FUCK YOU!

"Eh fuck you!" I replied.

"When, where, what time, and what position?" she asked.

"I don't want to know what you're asking your brother for sex again jenny." Mom said as she walked back in.

Ha!

Wait...

Where the hell did she get this "again"?

"When did I do it before?" she asked.

"I don't know, but knowing you, you probably have."

I just laughed.

The rest of the debate was stuff Jordan and I already knew, so we headed to my room to have a little bit of a make out session.

Yeah baby!

When I closed the door, I walked over to my bed where X was standing, hugged him, and started to make out like a couple of high schoolers.

I loved making out with him....

I lowered my hands to cover his butt, and he pushed me onto my bed. he crawled onto my bed, and lowered his lips to mine.

HIs divine lips...

The lips I never get sick of.

I pulled him down on me, and flipped him over. I trapped him, and started to kiss him.

He loved it when I did this.

He's more of the dominant nature, but he loved it when I tried to dominate him every once in a while.

I could feel his junk pushing into me.

I decided to tease him a little.

I pulled my head up, and let him just lay there as I went back down.

"You like teasing me, do you?" he asked.

"Hell yeah."

He flipped me over on my back, and spread my legs open. I thought he was going to blow a Connor on me.

You know...Fuck me...

But I was wrong.

He started to just feel me at first, but when I thought he was going to get serious, he stopped and kissed me for a while.

"Not fair!" I whiled a little.

"You deserve it." he replied and started to make out with me again.

I was sky high as usual. I liked it when he did this stuff with me.

But when I heard a voice from the door, I feel down like skydiving without a parachute.

"Boy I know what you're doing in their....He's giving you some of that GOOOOD HEEEAADDD!" Jenny said throughout under the door.

I picked up my shoe, and threw it at my door.

And she went off laughing.

God damnit....

"Where were we?" I asked as I lowered his face to mine.

But as we started, my phone rang.

"Why the fuck is it?" I asked and picked up my phone.

Paul...

"hello?" I answered.

"Hey Gary, I need to let you know that they took you out of the system."

WHAT?!

"What?!" I yelled. "Seriously?!"

"Yup. They're going to have an unexpected board meeting soon, and I think it's going to discuss about this situation."

I looked at X, and asked, "Is it open to students?"

"Yes."

"I'll have one of my friends go, and spy on them. Just in case."

"OK, but we're going to report on this anyway. I have to go. The President is calling."

"OK."

He hung up, and X asked, "What was *that* for?"

"They fired me from the school newspaper and they might talk about why at the next board meting. Since I'm not a student anymore -- they dropped my only class -- I need you to go and spy."

"When is it?"

"Monday."

"What do I get out of it?" he asked.

I Walked over to him, and felt his chest. I kissed him, and said, "Maybe some fun."

"I'll take that for free any day of the week."

CHAPTER 17

Jordan decided that he wanted dot stay the night at my place, and I let him. We haven't had a sleepover in a while.

I missed it.

And I didn't have to work OR go to school the next morning!

SUNDAY!

The only day I was off…

When I woke up, I felt X's hand across my chest, and his face smudged into my shoulder.

He was sound asleep.

I twisted around, and cuddled with him.

The hogged the entirety of the damn covers last night, and it left me freezing!

That's the bad part about sleeping with him.

I kissed him on the nose, and closed my eyes.

"Good morning." he whispered.

Damn…

He's awake…

"Good morning." I whispered back and kissed him.

He wrapped his arm around my back and pushed me in as we made out. he slid his hand down my back, and put his hand on my butt.

I half the back of his head, and stared to make out with him.

"It's too early for you guys to be making out!" Jenny moaned.

I let go, and looked at her standing in the doorway, in her Pajamas.

"You're lucky mom's gone to church." she replied.

"Why you always try into get into our sex life?" X asked.

"Well, I'm warning you because mom is on her way home." she said and closed the door. "You're welcome!"

Mom hates it when we cuddle.

Yeah, she accepts that I'm gay, but she's still a hardcore republican.

She is against homosexuality.

And she hates sex. ever since my father abandoned us, she has hated it.

but that's her problem.

X got dressed, and we had are last minute kiss before he left.

I watched as he drove off, and went into the morning traffic.

I'm so lucky to have someone like him!

I walked back to my room, and got on some clothes.
I went over to my computer, and went to Facebook.

And I got a surprising message from Roman.

I GOT COURT PAPERS! I'M NOT EVEN FUCKING JOKING! HE'S SUEING US!

WHAT?!

I rushed out to my mailbox, and pulled what seemed to be a letterform the state.

Yup...

I got it too...

For "Disturbing the peace"

Suck my cock you Bitch Lasagna!

Wait...

Eww!

I don't want a daddy!

I ran to my room, and typed back that I got it too.

While we were talking about the situation, Mom knocked on my door.

"What's this about disturbing the peace? Is this from that professor?" she asked.

SHIT!

I left it on the kitchen table!

"Yes, he is suing me and Roman for saying our opinion." I replied.

She looked at me, and took out her phone. She dialed a familiar number, and then said, "Hey Rick, this is Gary's mother. We have a problem that we need your help with."

CHAPTER 18
ONE WEEK LATER.

I was assigned by Mary's secretary to write up a press release and submit it to the Oak Tree Times. They already know that I'm writing the article, and I just have to submit it to them.

When I wrote the last word, Roman came into the newsroom.

We were still allowed in here -- we would be working for free -- because they hardly have any editors...

"So, how's the article for the Oak Tree times coming along?" He asked.

"Good." I replied. I printed out the document, and sat on the couch to do the edits.

Roman sat down at his computer, and started to print out a lot of pages.

"Damn, that's a lot of trees being killed. "I stated.

"Well, that's the court papers. I don't know where a lawyer is for us. I've been searching all week..." he replied and rubbed his hands on his face.

I turned around, and looked into his emerald eyes. "I have one planned for us."

He sprung his face up, and asked, "WHO?!"

"Rick Louis."

His eyes opened wide. "You mean, *the* rick Louis? The Rick Louis that has *never* lost a case?"

"Yup."

His face grew a smile. "YES! We're goanna win!"

"O, and I have my boyfriend going to the board meeting to spy on them. he'll record if they say anything about us, and give it to us for evidence."

"Yes!" he cheered. "We're SO going to win!"

"Is it possible we can ask for a libertarian judge? Maybe that will increase our chances for wining."

"I don't know. If we can, we're in for the jackpot.

***

Later that night, we were gathered around the TV again.

it was the second round for the debates.

There were rumors that Phill Pozman won't be there.

I think he's going to drop out of the race.

If he does, I hope they don't choose anyone else.

We don't need a democrat in our office...Like, ever...

When the newscast sopped flapping their gums, they stared the second debate.

"Good evening and welcome to the second of three presidential debates between the leading candidates for president of the United States. The democrat Nominee, Phill Pozman couldn't make it tonight due to reasons. The candidates for this debate are the Republican nominee, President Jarmen McMiller, and the Libertarian nominee, Marry Stone."

I KNEW IT!

Now we have to wait until he drops out.

"My name is Carole Simpson, and I will be the moderator for tonight's 90-minute debate, which is coming to you from the campus of Lindenwood University in St. Louis, Missouri now, tonight's program is unlike any other presidential debate in history. We're making history now and it's pretty exciting. A third part will be debating against the republican nominee.

Now, representatives of both the Republican and Libertarian campaigns have agreed to the format, and there is no subject matter that is restricted. Anything goes. We can ask anything.

After the debate, the candidates will have an opportunity to make a closing statement. So, President Jarmen, I think you said it earlier…"

"Let's do this thing!" Jarmen replied.

God…

"And I think the first question is over here."

Oh!

This is the one where they ask questions from the audience!"

Good!

AUDIENCE QUESTION: Yes. I'd like to direct my question to Ms. Stone. I have a twin brother who has a business at the age of 20. He imports things from China, and sells them over 200% of the original price. How will you stop this and bring jobs back here in our own country?"

Wow…

A 20o year old with a business.

Impressive.

"First off congratulations for your brother, and that's right at the top of my agenda. We source our products from overseas to sell here, we're not creating American jobs. They want to do this because of costs. It's so much cheaper to make a necklace in China, then here.

If I were elected president, I would give tax cuts to those people who switch. Not 10%. Not 20%. Not 30%. And not 40% I will do 50% tax cuts to those companies. That is how we stop sourcing from china.

Is to give them more money to buy our American products. Thank you for the amazing question ma'am."

Wow!

That's sort of evil, but clever!

What if the item is $10, and you have to sell it for $20?

Not right Mary!

SIMPSON: Thank you, Ms. Stone. I see that the president has stood up, so he must have something to say about this.

"We need to do something about it. You're right! In my second term, I will raise taxes to those who do source from china. I will raise it 200%, and whoever sources from here, they will get a 20% tax break."

What…the…fuck…

Evil motherfucker!

"Thank you president. I think we have another question over here."

While the question was being asked, I could hear mom get up from the couch, and walk off.

angry…

I followed her, and looked in her room.

"Everything ok?" I asked.

"I just can't believe our leader is such an ass hole!" she complained. "This next four years is going to be hell!"

Not if Mary get's elected.

and I have a strong feeling this will.

CHAPTER 19
Nov. 9, 2016

Well, today was the day.

Today was the day that we vote for the president of the United States.

Mary is FOR SURE going to win!

I hope…

There is one person who could get in the way though.

Eddie Mackerlock.

He is an independent, and he is popular in his own state, as well as a couple others.

His plan is to deadlock the Electoral College, send it to the House, and win.

He won't though!

I hope...

I headed to First god Church near our hose, to go vote.

When I showed my ID, I headed to the electronic voting booth, and they set me up.

and there it was….

```
( ) Republican:
Jarmen McMiller: (P)
Vince Gerroold (VP)


( ) Democratic
Phill Pozzman (P)
Kasandra Karted (VP)


( ) Libertarian:
Mary Stone: (P)
Patience Ashmad (VP)


( ) Write in:
_____(P)
_____(VP)
```

There's only one choice for this election.

Mary.

I clicked Mary's name, and proceeded to fill out the rest of the form. It was stuff like our representatives, our senators, and some Supreme Court Judges.

Stuff I just voted Libertarian on.

When I was done, I double-checked that I voted for Mary, and submitted my vote.

There we go.

I have officially voted for the first time.

And I have never been so proud in my entire life.

I exited the church, and got into my car with a smile.

We were going to win this thing!

***

It was almost six, and I had to write an opinion piece and post it on the Gossip's website on who I voted for, why, and who I think will win. I was halfway done with the piece, when Jenny busted into my room.

Damm girl!

"Yes?" I asked.

"Time to see the results!"

YES!

I rushed out to the living room, and I was Happier than a motherfucker!

"We're calling both states -- Indiana and Kentucky -- will go to Mary Stone. We're predicting this is going to be a tight race. Don't you think?" the news anchor asked the others.

"Yes, I think Pozman might win, because of the fact we have two right wingers, and one left winger. it would split the right side."

"Don't forget about Marlock, the left wing independent. He seems to be leading in multiple polls in multiple states."

The other anchor looked pissed.

"Let's us agree to disagree," she said.

Damn!

"We can't do that because of the facts." they replied.

Damn right!

Facts over feelings!

"Well, let's head over to the Jarmen Publicist, and ask their opinion on this subject."

Fuck, I hate that campaign!

I got up, and walked to my room.

I didn't want to deal with that bullshit.

when I got back into my room, I looked at my Facebook, and saw a message from roman.

** I'm predicting the court date won't be for another year.**

Good!
I replied to his message, and continued on my article.

***

When I was done with the article around eight, I headed out of my room, and I found Mom and Jenny watching TV.

"What's the status?" I asked and sat down.

"Have a look."

I looked at the screen, and noticed that MARY WAS WINNING!

She had 189 fucking Electoral College votes!

Missouri, Kansas, Texas, and a lot more!

WOW!

As I was waiting for the news anchors to shut up about their opinions, to stop, I got a call from Jordan.

"What's up?" I asked.

"Come over." he replied.

"But I'm watching the results." I replied.

"But my parents aren't home."

Well, there I go!

I got up and grabbed my keys.

"Where you going?" mom asked.

"Jordan's house."

"Use protection." Jenny said and laughed.

"Safe sex is good sex." Mom added on.

Eww...

Not after Connor...

"Y'all suck." I replied and walked out.

CHAPTER 20

I walked into Jordan's room with him, and I sat down on his bed.

"Why am I here?" I asked.

He pushed me down on the bed, and kissed me. "You promised this after I went to the meeting, sexy."

That's right!

Well, I'm not goanna say no!

I pulled him down closer to me, and madly made out with him.

Those never got old.

He grasped my hands, and pinned me down so I couldn't move. he stared to kiss down my chest, and stared to kiss my junk.

I didn't think I would, but I accidently jerked my junk and hit him in the mouth.

"You want to play that way bad boy?" he asked.

"Yes baby."

he pulled down my pants, and looked at my penis.

"Damn, haven't had this in a while."

Damn!

I haven't had this since Connor devoured me.

He then stared to rub his hands over me.

"Want to cuddle?" he asked.

"Yes."

***

I woke up about midnight from a call from Jenny.

"Hello?" I asked, tired.

"You guys did it!"

I was confused.

"Who's that?" X asked.

I put her on speakerphone, and said, "Jordan's here."

"Hey shrimp dick." she replied.

"I don't have a damn shrimp dick!" he replied. "I'm joking. But anyway, Mary got enough Electoral College votes that there taking it to the House of Representatives!"

WHAT?

That woke me up!

"WHAT?!" I asked. Surprised.

"YES! They might choose her, because they're mostly Republican!"

YES!

"I'll let you two sleep." she said and hung up.

Jordan looked at me, and kissed me. "You did it baby."

~102~

I know.

I'm so proud!

"We need to celebrate." I whispered.

"I have the perfect idea." he said and pushed me on the bed.

PART THREE
THE COMEBACK

CHAPTER 22

"THE ENTIRE ELECTION WAS RIGGED!"

I've been hearing this all week...

The media saying Phill dropping out was a publicity stunt so Jarmen could win...

That the Libertarian party rigged the election.

And most of all, that we're not as free as we're saying.

I had a fuck load of interviews by CNN, Fox, and many other news outlets because of this, and I told them ALL the same thing.

"We'll have to wait for the House of Representatives to decide who is our next leader. For now, I plead the fifth."

There was nothing else I could say.

I DON'T know any of their answers.

"LOOK, this election was rigged because of those damn freedom loving libertarians!"

"NO! I know I'm no right wing Nazi like Jarmen, but the entire media predicted a Stone/Ashmad victory! You CAN'T say that, unless you think there fake news."

"YES! THEY ARE FAKE NEWS!"

OK, that's enough…

"EVERYONE SHUT UP! WE'RE NOT THREE YEAR OLDS! WE'RE ADULTS!"

That go them…

Good.

"Now, as I tell everyone else on the media. We'll have to wait for the house of representatives to decide who is our next leader."

"No! Jarmen IS the winner, and we'll prove it!" Jarmen's Campaign manager said and hung up."

There was a silence, and then I said, "Well, I better get going."

Nobody was there…

The green party Campaign manager must have hung up…

I hung up the phone, and sat it on my bed. Jordan was sitting on my bed, looking at me with wide eyes.

"Holy crap! I have NEVER seen you get that angry!" he said and pated on the back.

"I know. But they got me worked up." I replied and turned around, I sat next to him on the bed, and looked ta him. "I'm a little worried."

"Why?"

"Not only do I have the lawsuit with that damn professor, but I also might have one with the Stone/Ashmad campaign.

He kissed me, and whispered, "I want to make your worries go away."

I pushed him away, ad laid on my bed. "Jordan, not now."

He laid next to me, and said, "Well, I promise you it'll be ok."

He cuddled beside me, and I started to feel better.

His touch always felt good.

"Let's just sleep on it. You'll feel better when you wake up."

CHAPTER 23

I walked into the newsroom the next day, tired.

Jordan wouldn't stop moving in his sleep.

I love the guy, but I need my beauty sleep!

I sat down on my computer, and pulled up the web browser. I meant to type in my email client, but accidently typed in MSNBC.com

How the fuck did I manage that?

But the title woke me up.

Jarmen's team requests hand count in all states Mary Stone won

OH NO THEY DON'T

I swear, if they do a manual recount of ALL of the states, we will NEVER be able to see Mary in the oval office.

I dialed Mary's phone and waited.

"Hey Gary, did you hear?" she asked.

"About the recount? Yeah." I replied.

"Well, I say that we need to let him do the recount. They have no proof of a rigged election, because there was none. The people voted for us, and we won fair an square."

True...

And if anything, it Might prove voter fraud against the greens or the democrats. Maybe both."

"I honestly think that one of Missouri's electoral votes were rigged, along with the entire state of Florida and the deep south. We had a strong lead in those states. We need to get a recount in those states."

That's right!

I remember seeing that that BOTH states predicted that Mary would be their winner!

But no.

Jarmen was.

"Request it! And while you're at it, request Maine. I have the strangest feeling those two electoral college votes go to us."

"OK, I'll talk to ya later." She said and hung up.

When I hung up, I noticed Roman was watching me...

"So, you guys are doing a recount too?" he asked.

"Yup." Might as well get back at him like he's trying to steal our victory."

CHAPTER 24

** Hey, wanna hangout? **

X had texted me that in the middle of our meeting, and when we were done, I knew the answer to *that*.

It's a hell yeah!

When I arrived at his house, he let me in, and I sat down on his couch. He was watching TV.

"So, how was your day?" he asked and kissed my neck.

"Boring. You gave me something when you texted me." I said and winked.

He smiled, and laid his hand on my leg. He leaned in, and stared to make out with me.

Kisses with him were fucking amazing.

I mean, who doesn't love a good kiss?

Nobody!

I laid on top of him, and grabbed his hands, one went in the couch, and the other went behind his head.

He seemed to enjoy it.

I lifted me head away from his lips, and said, "Let's cuddle."

"You don't want to make out anymore?"

I *always* want are you talking about?

I want to make out with you!

Like…. always!

"No, I feel like cuddling with you." I replied.

I lay down on the couch, and he laid his head on my chest.

***

He was sleeping on my chest.

He slept like a little baby.

I didn't mind.

As long as I was with him.

I tried to be as quiet as possible, but when my phone rang, I wanted to punch whoever called me.

Roman.

This better be good!

"Hello?" I whispered.

"He dropped the charges!"

"Who?"

"That damn professor!"

WHAT?!

YES!

I could feel Jordan's head slowly float off my chest, and he looked at me. "What is it?"

"Thanks." I said and hung up. "The charges were dropped!"

"From Jarmen?"

I wish!

"No, the professor pressing charges against us!"

He looked at me, rubbed his eyes, and smiled. "Good. Wanna celebrate?"

"I can't. I open tomorrow."

He frowned. "Damnit."

CHAPTER 25
ONE WEEK LATER

I hated opening at this damn place!

I had to open by myself for a long time. It was hard. I had to count all the drawers, prepare ALL the food, take all the orders, do ALL the prep, and fry everything.

Sometimes, I would have Tammy come with me, but this time, she couldn't.

She was working all night on a school project, and didn't get any sleep.

I know how that feels!

So I don't blame her!

When I parked in the store parking lot, I noticed that she WAS there.

Want the fuck?

She was standing there on her phone!

I walked out of my car, and walked up to her. "So, how was the project?"

"I got done with it early, and decided to help you with truck. You're welcome."

Thanks booboo!

We opened the doors, and looked at the back.

Holy...shit...

There were more boxes than I thought!

When I opened the walk-in, boxes fell down in front of me. I had to scoot out of the way because I was afraid of being smashed.

Great...

That's all I need...

I took a deep breath, and looked at Tammy. She looked like she was about to laugh.

But holding it back.

Because she knows better.

"Fuck this." I commented.

"Can I cry now?" se asked.

"Not until we get this truck done." I replied and stared on the walk-in.

***

Vince came in a while later, and right when he entered, it was like rush had already run loose.

It was Me, Tammy, Vince, and some new guy who is useless as fuck.

He's been here for two months, and still doesn't know jack shit.

He was always calling me to help him, and when I did, they looked at him with anger.

"I'm sorry ma'am, but first off, do *not* call us a shithole, and second, if you harass anyone else here, we will kick you out. Understand?"

"This guy is outrageous! This little cunt here is a fucking retard!" She yelled, making a scene.

"Excuse me you little piece of shit. You do NOT call any of my employees any profound names. And second off, what is your name?"

"Why do you need to know you faggot?"

"Because you are banned from this store!" Vince said as he waked in.

"You know what, I'm reporting you to corporate!" she yelled and stormed out.

In looked at Keith, and said. "We're franchise, but oh well." and walked off to the kitchen.

I rejoined Tammy and put some gloves on. She was going faster than the speed of light, and looked like she was going to burst out into tears at any moment in time.

"Breath Tammy." I said and joined her. I rolled up a burrito, and put it in a bag. "Breath."

That was the breaking point.

She busted into tear, and went to the office.

Great…

She always has panic attacks when it's a HUGE rush like this.

And I don't blame her.

It's VERY stressful!

I tried to comfort her, while making food at the name time.

CHAPTER 26

When the rush was over with, I got myself a drink of Mountain Dew, and went to the office. I sat down on the desk, and started to count the new guys drawer.

"So, how is he doing with his training?" Vince asked.

I finished counting the drawer, and said, "Well first, he's ten dollars short, and second, he doesn't know jack shit!"

Vince's eyes went wide. "Ten DOLLARS?!"

"Yup."

Vince recounted my work, and said, "No, it's twenty!"

Great...

Before Vince took his phone an called his manager, I got a call from Mary.

"Hello, president elect." I greeted.

"hey, do you know Tammy Louis?"

"Yeah, why?"

"Well, I know her father is a lawyer, and I was going to ask him if we could use him for this case. He has NEVER lost a case, and we could use him to defend us."

Smart idea.

Why couldn't I have through of that?!

"tammy is here, so let me get in contact with her." I said and put her on mute. "TAMMY! GET YOUR BUTT OBVER HERE!"

Tammy obeyed, and walked over to me. "Yes?"

I unmuted the phone, and handed it to her.

Tammy went into the break room, and when I got done with some manager stuff, she came back.

"I have her my dad's number to see, and you got a message from someone in Grindr."

"You weren't supposed to see that." I replied and snatched my phone.

"I didn't want to see the dick pic some old guy send me." she replied.

EWW!

These older guys are all on me for some reason!

Probably because I'm in college…

***

After an *intense* makeout session with Jordan later that night, we were cuddling, watching Fox News.

I didn't want to watch MSNBC or CNN.

They're a bunch of lib-tards...

When it started, Shannon Bream was on screen.

"She's so hot." Jordan said.

"Boy! You're gay!"

"That doesn't mean I can call a woman hot."

"While we were debating with the TV on, I heard an interruption.

About Mary.

"Shut up!" I demanded. "I heard something about Mary!"

"The Supreme court has decided that Mary Stone is now the president-elect of the United States of America."

ABOUT THE AUTHOR

Bestselling author Ian Schrauth was born in St. Louis, MO. He is currently attending Maricopa Community College, where he is working towards his degree in Computer science. In addition, he is a former Software Developer for one of the largest internet companies in the United States.

Ian currently lives in Mehlville, Missouri.

Additional information can be found on his website.

www.ianschrauth.com
www.facebook.com/AuthorIanSchrauth
www.instagram.com/authorianschrauth
www.tiktok.com/@author_ian_schrauth